The Big Cheese Family

Book 1: *"Not'cho Cheese!"*

Written by Tony Jerris

Illustrated by Oliver Batin

DEDICATION

For the cheese lovers in all of us, big or small.

ACKNOWLEDGMENTS

Tony and Oliver would like to thank their respective families and friends for their continued support, including Renee Batin, Mickey and Nelson Batin, Corinne Aquilina, Dave Elliott and Ann Jerris.

The *Big Cheese Family* lives in a store,
Inside a nook near the back door.

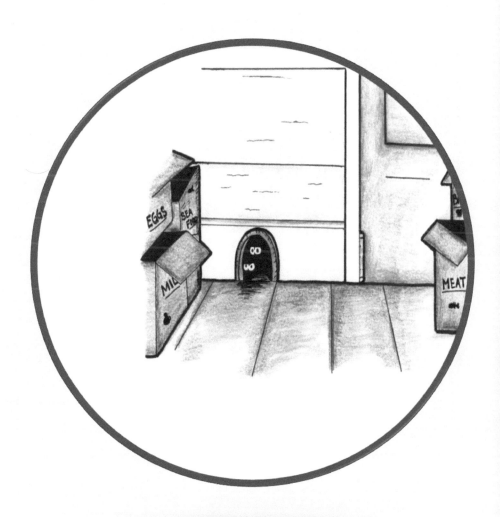

The store's filled with food that is sure to please,
But this family of mice loves only cheese!

There's Papa Parmesan. He's married to Brie.

Brie's having a baby.

Maybe two. Could be three.

Their other kids are grown and have left the nest,
Except for Reggiano, who at times is a pest.

It's not that he's mean. He's actually quite nice.
Though he often ignores his father's advice.
"Stay away from the traps," Papa warns his son,
Before he ventures out to have some fun.

Still, Reggiano gets too close to a trap,
That suddenly springs shut with a very loud snap.

"My tail!" the mouse shrieks. "Papa, I'm stuck!"
Papa races to the scene of his son's bad luck.

While lifting the spring, Papa scolds his boy,
"What did I tell you? This isn't a toy!"

"Sorry, Papa," Reggiano replies.
"From now on I promise to play inside."

"It's okay," Papa says. "Be more careful next time,
And *always* stay clear of Mr. McGrime."

Mr. McGrime is the grocery store owner.
He's cranky and old, and somewhat of a loner.

Day after day, he tries catching the mice,
And has nearly succeeded once or twice.

But the mice are quick-- Too quick for McGrime.
As he reaches for them, up the walls the mice climb.

"You're driving me mad!" McGrime's voice roars.

Frightened customers make a dash for the doors.

"Come back!" McGrime pleads. "I'm under attack,
By a family of mice who live in thc back!"

Meanwhile, back inside the *'Mouse House,'*
Brie cooks, and cleans and irons her blouse.

Grandpa Gouda is coming for dinner tonight,
And Brie wants everything to be just right.

Grandpa Gouda is widowed and spends his time,
Traveling the globe for less than a dime,
By hopping on busses or jumping on trains.

He's even snuck rides on a few airplanes.

When Grandpa arrives, dinner is set,
But when Brie looks in the oven, she starts to fret.

The mac-and-cheese she made earlier that day
Has mysteriously vanished in some strange way.

Where did it go? Brie thinks to herself.

It couldn't have just walked off by itself.

Reggiano finally confesses the truth:
"I ate it," he adds, "and it's stuck in my tooth."

Papa and Brie shoot Reggiano a look.
Grandpa chimes in, "Let's get out of this nook."

The others follow Grandpa into the store,
As Mr. McGrime hangs a sign in the door.

The sign reads "Closed," and the mice all smile.
With everyone gone, they can play for awhile.

They partied all night, feasting on cheese...

'Til their bellies were full and sunk to their knees.

Come morning, when McGrime reopened his shop,
His eyes grew wide before blowing his top.

"It's not'cho cheese!" McGrime tugged at his hair.

But the mice were asleep…

… Without a care.

It's an ongoing game of mice and man.
Maybe one day McGrime will devise a plan,
To catch the mice and reclaim what is his.

Until that time comes, it is what it is.

CHEESE GLOSSARY

PARMESAN: A hard Italian aged cow's milk cheese.

BRIE: A soft cow's milk cheese named after a region in France.

REGGIANO: A hard granular cheese named after Parma, Italy.

GOUDA: A pale yellow Dutch cheese.

SAGE: A cheese flavored with sage and colored by spinach leaves.

MUENSTER: A semisoft cheese made from whole milk.

FETA: A crumbly, salty Greek cheese made from sheep's or goats milk.

MANCHEGO: A sheep's milk cheese from Spain.

SWISS: A medium-hard yellow cheese with a lot of holes.

BLUE: A soft cheese with greenish-blue mold and a strong flavor.

ABOUT THE AUTHOR

Tony Jerris is an accomplished playwright, author and screenwriter. His off-Broadway play TELL VERONICA! ran in New York City before premiering in Los Angeles. As an author, Tony created a trilogy of children's books. The first in the series, *The Littlest Spruce*, was featured on Good Morning America. The third book, *The Littlest Witch*, he adapted into a musical that is being licensed by Steele Spring Licensing. His book "Marilyn Monroe: My Little Secret" has been featured on *Extra-TV!* and he has written a new stop-motion feature film called The Potters with JenKev Productions. Tony currently lives in Los Angeles where he has other film projects in development.

ABOUT THE ILLUSTRATOR

Oliver Batin is an artist from Omaha, Nebraska. His father, Nelson Batin, is a professional artist, so as a kid, art ran through Oliver's blood. Every morning as a child he loved getting up to watch his favorite cartoon, *Teenage Mutant Ninja Turtles*, which inspired him to draw the characters. In school, Oliver had a 4th Grade reading level that he struggled with up until the 10th Grade. And while his teachers told his parents that every kid must learn the same way, Oliver's parents knew that he was a visual learner, encouraging him to pursue his dreams no matter what other people thought of him. Over the years, Oliver has place various drawing competitions and is now drawing full-time. He is happy to be working with author Tony Jerris, and lives by the motto: "Never give up no matter what life throws in your path, and always use the talents that God's given you."

CPSIA information can be obtained
at www.ICGtesting.com
Printed in the USA
LVHW071559201219
641251LV00001B/4/P